The Snowman

Illustrated by Stella Yang

Rigby

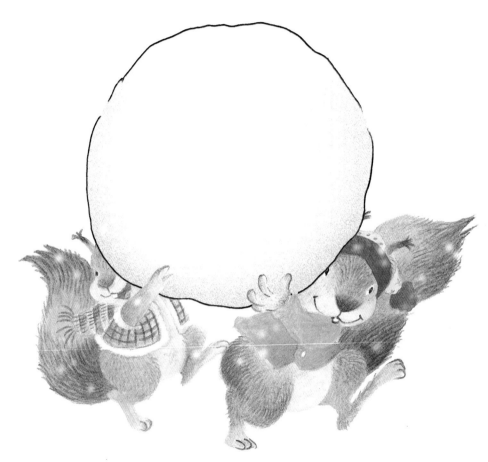

We put on
the head.

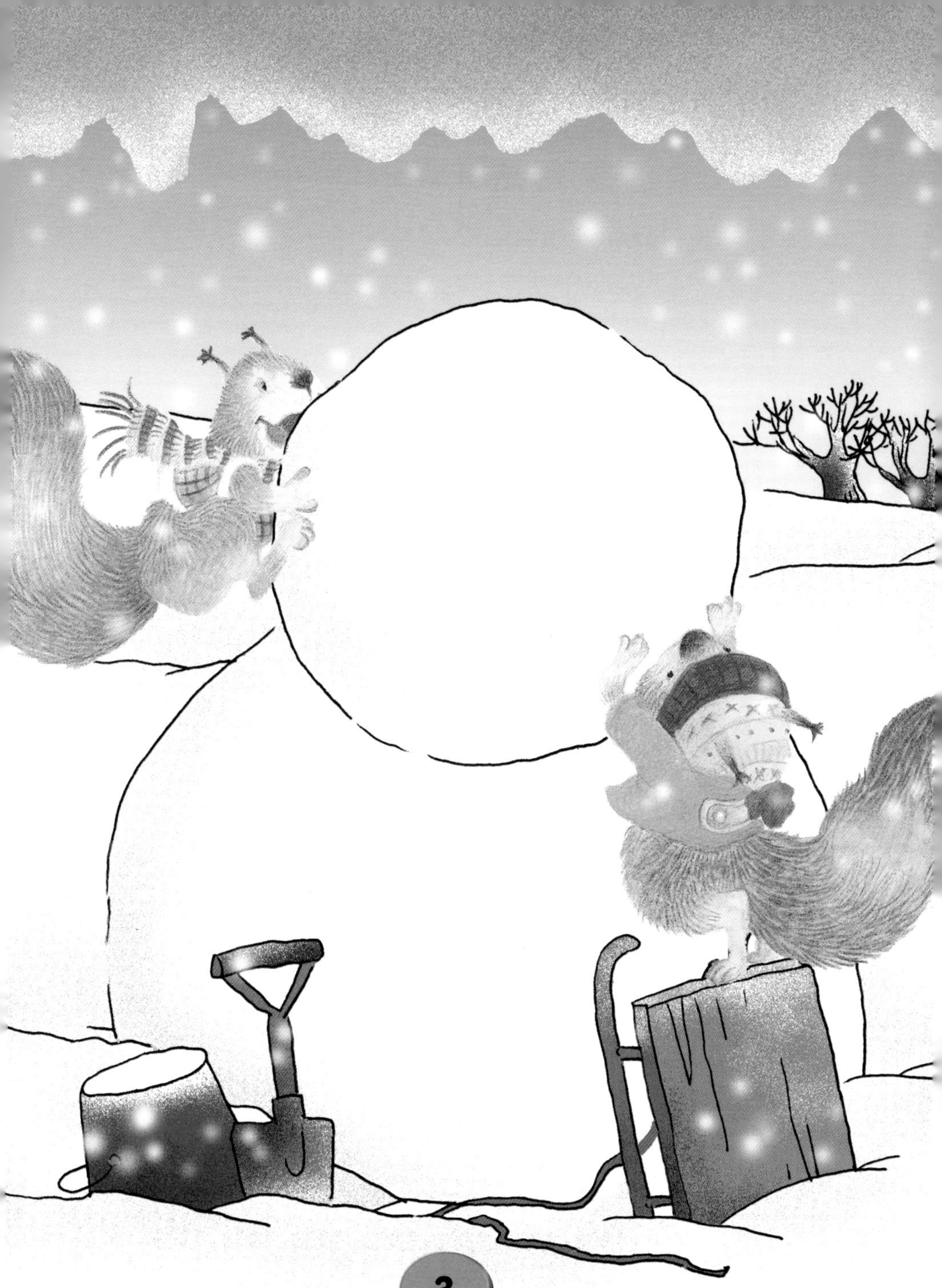

We put on
the eyes.

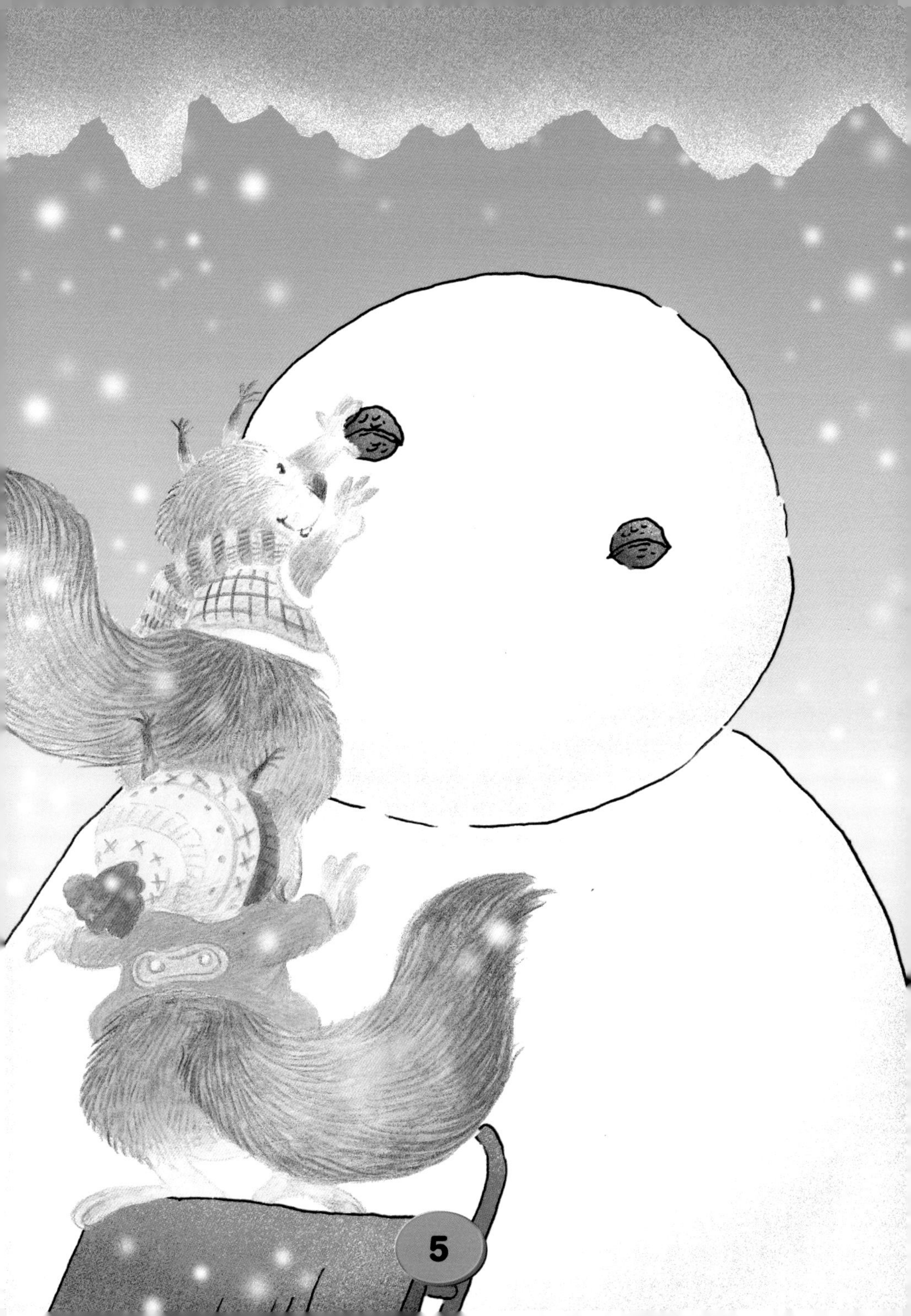

We put on
the mouth.

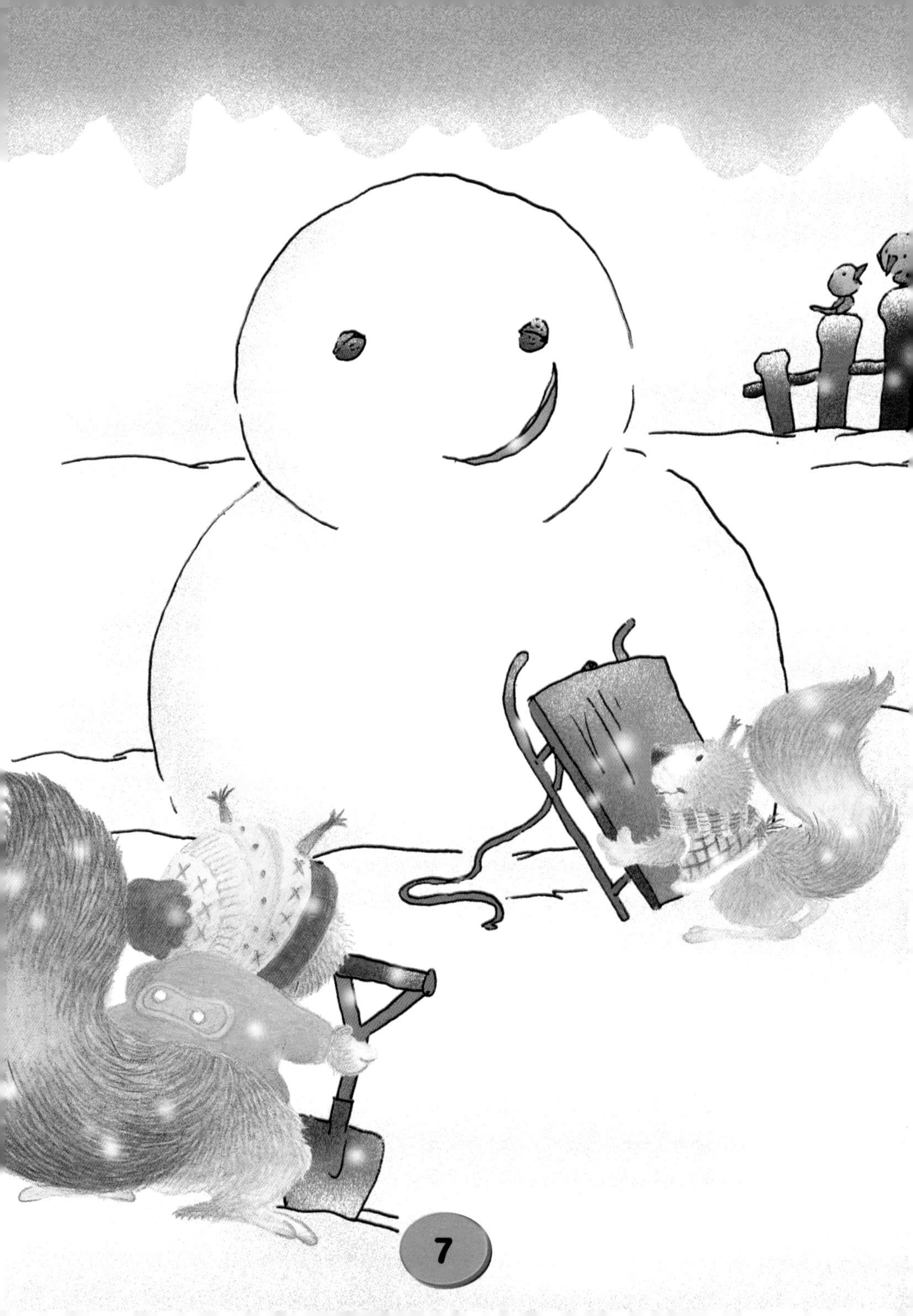

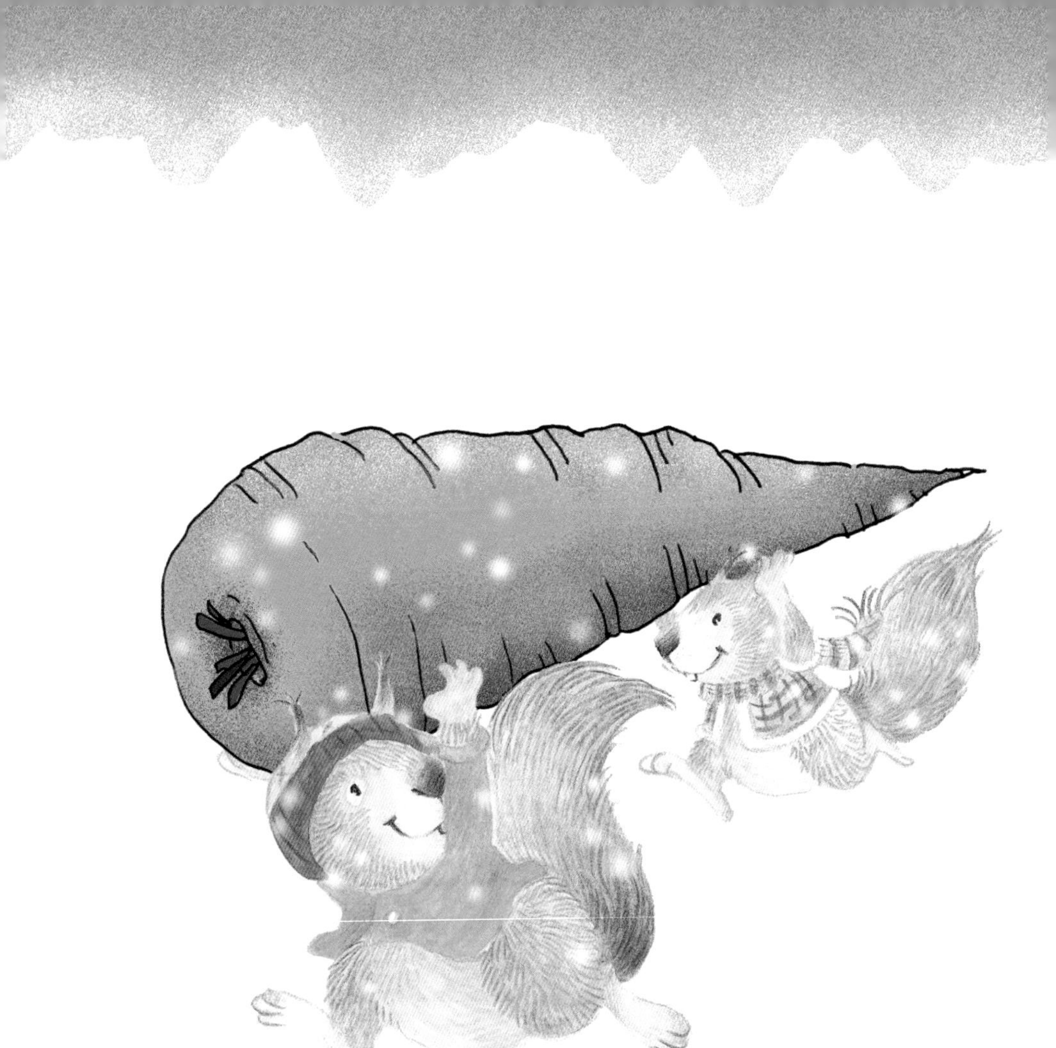

We put on
the nose.

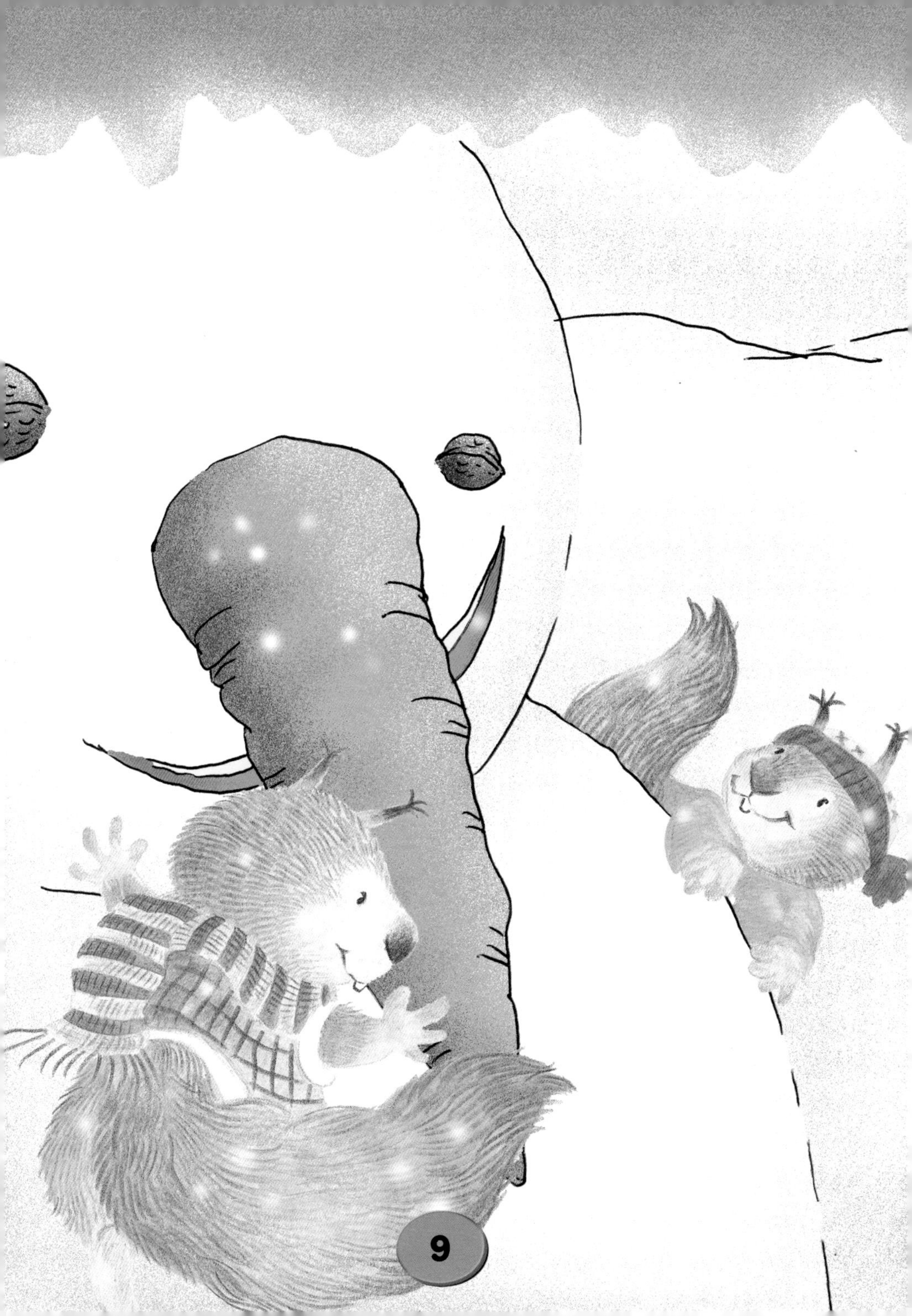

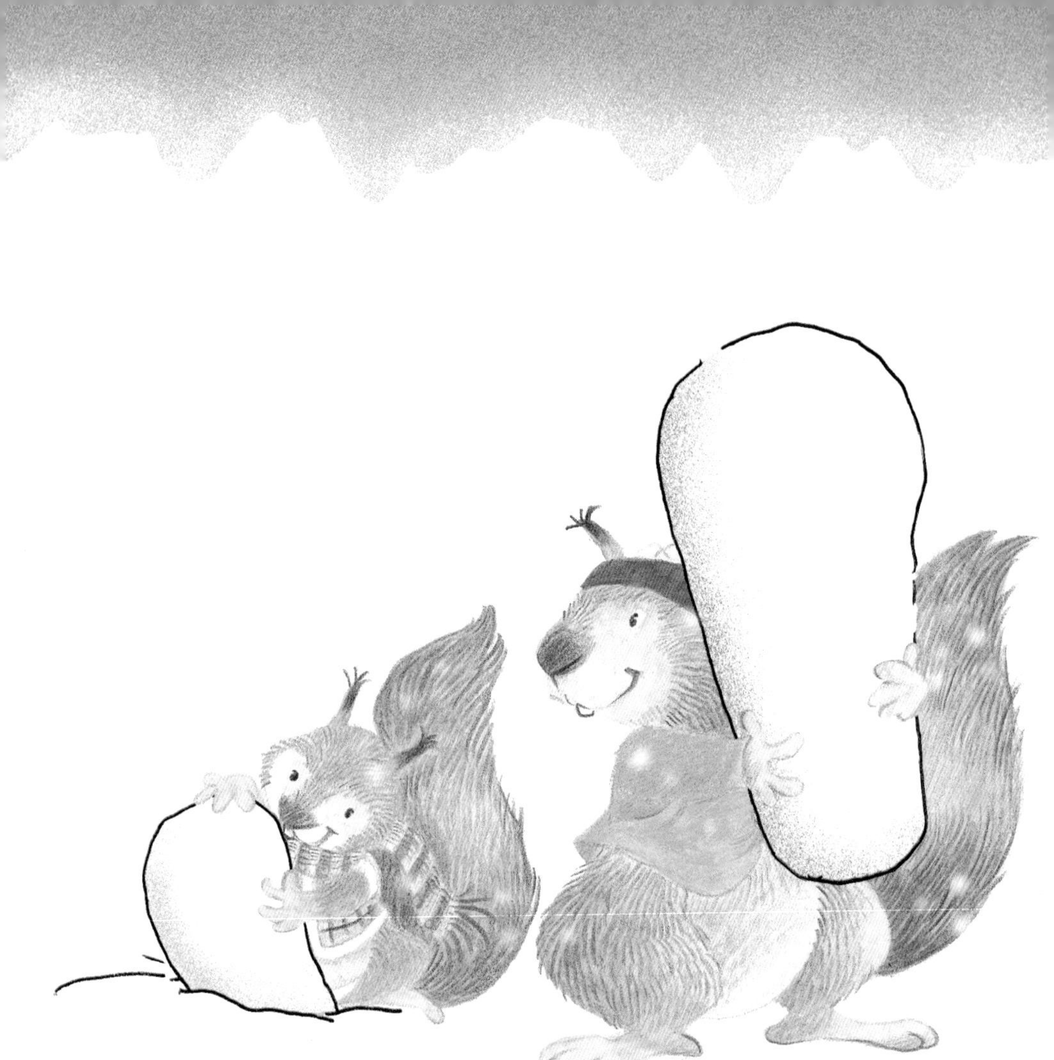

We put on
the arms.

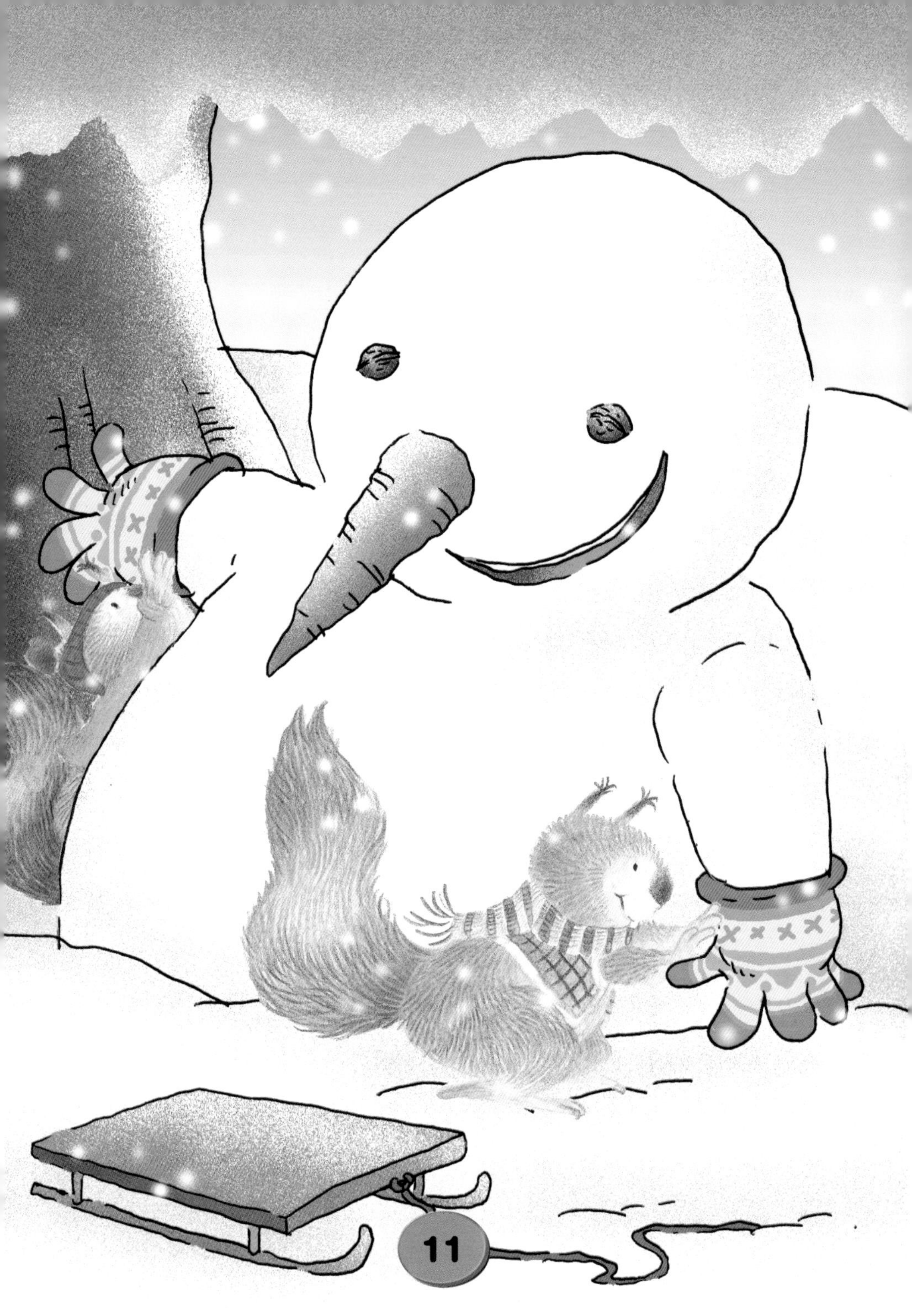

We put on
the hat.

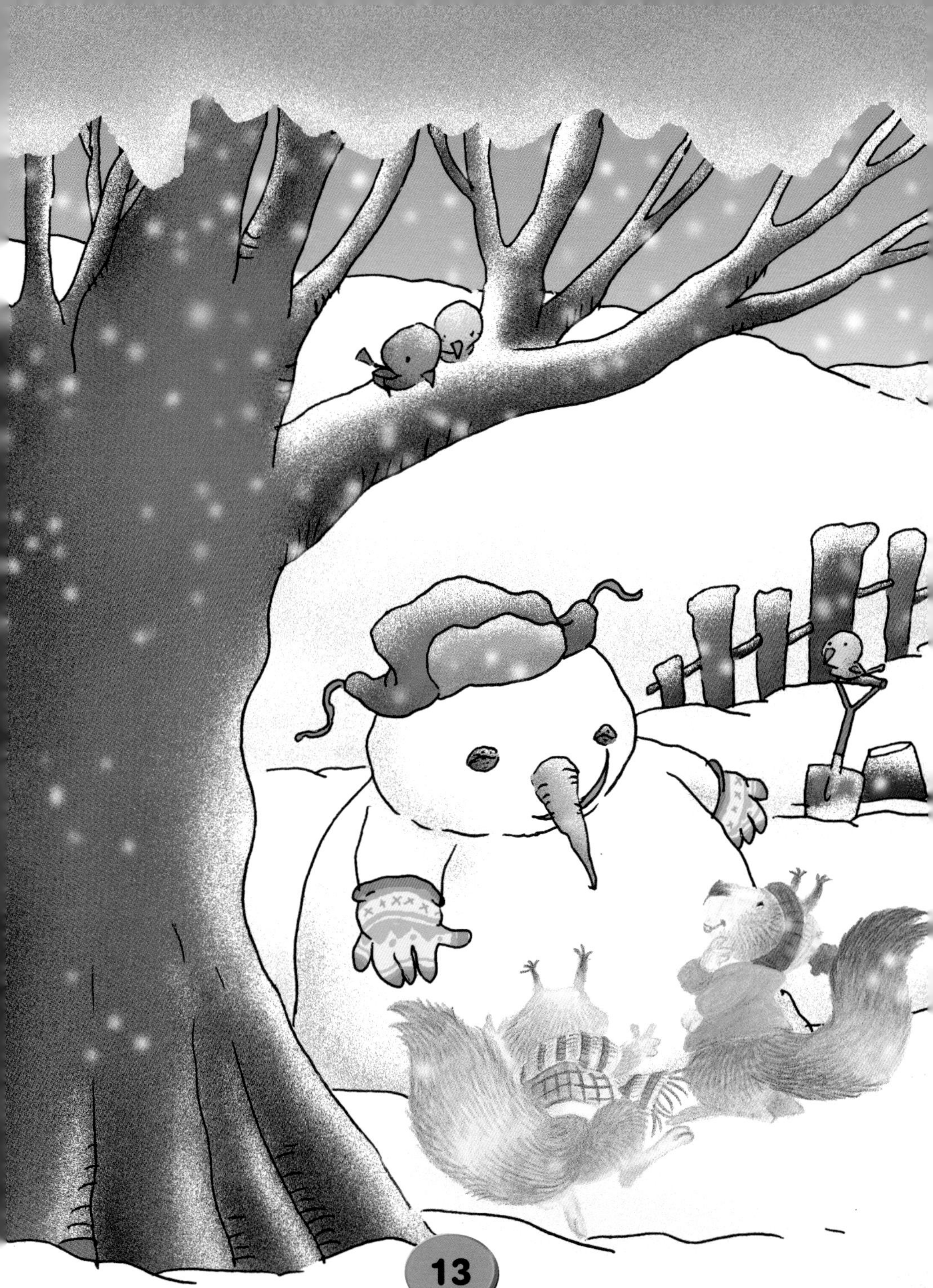

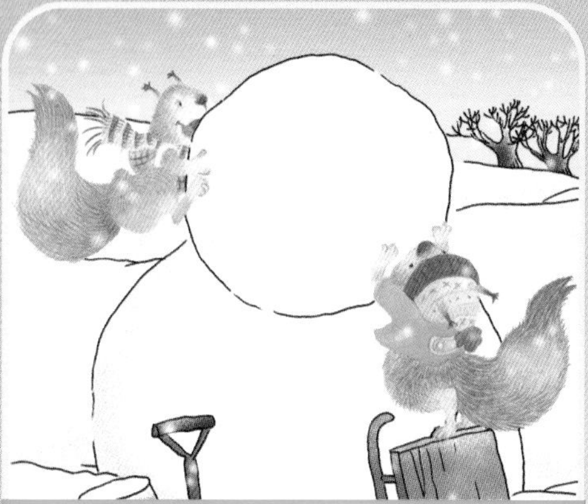

We put on the head.

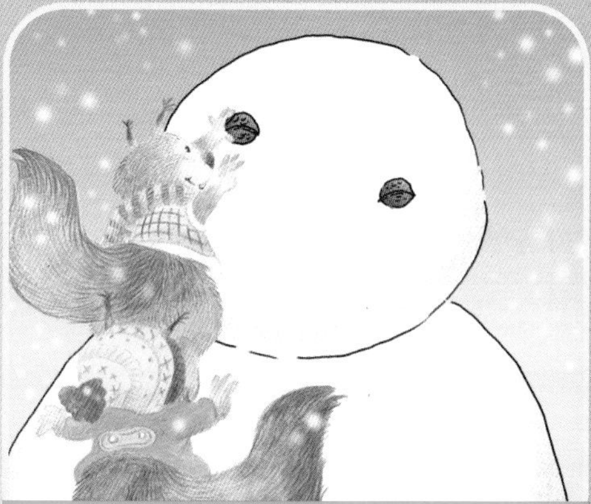

We put on the eyes.

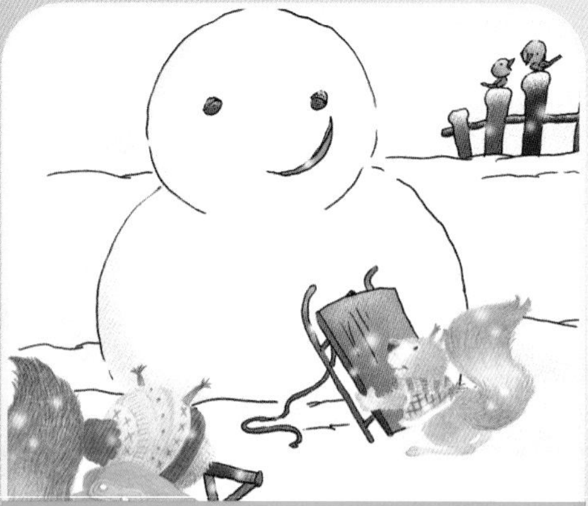

We put on the mouth.

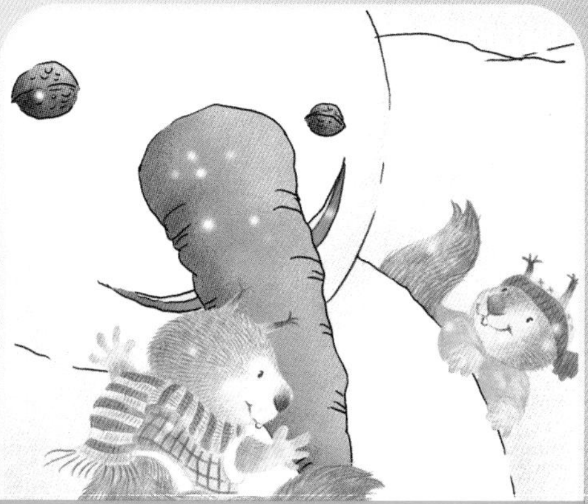

We put on the nose.

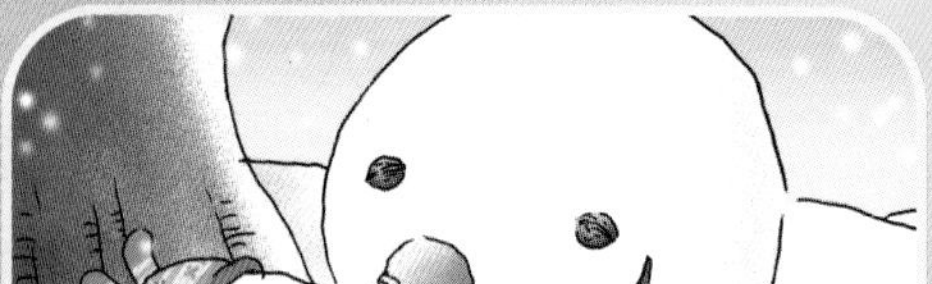

We put on the arms.

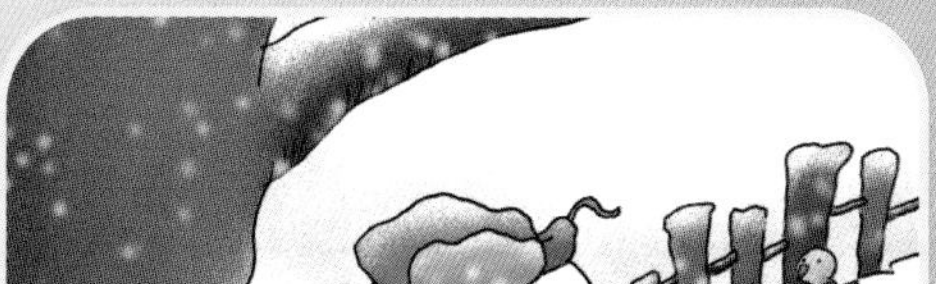

We put on the hat.

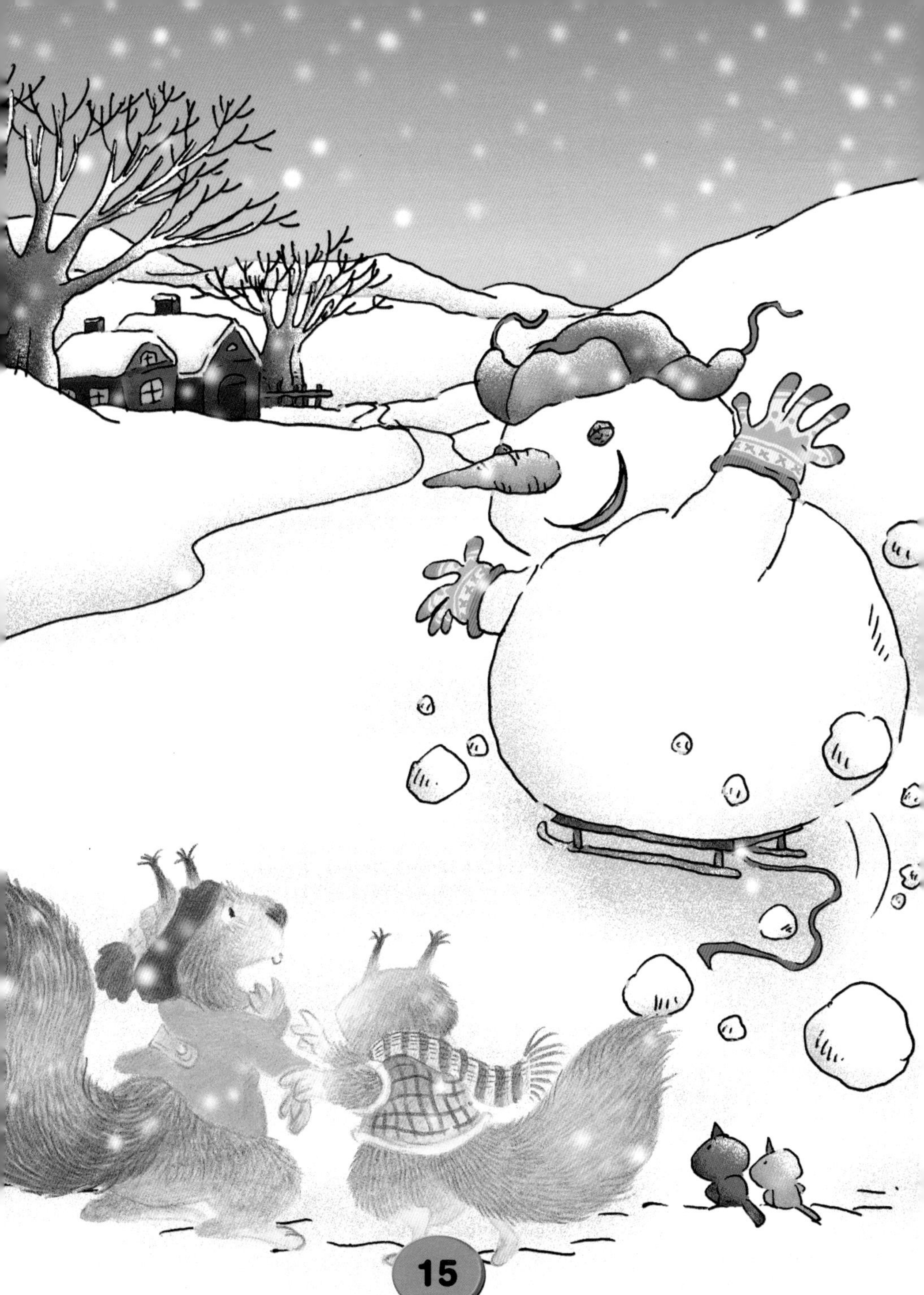

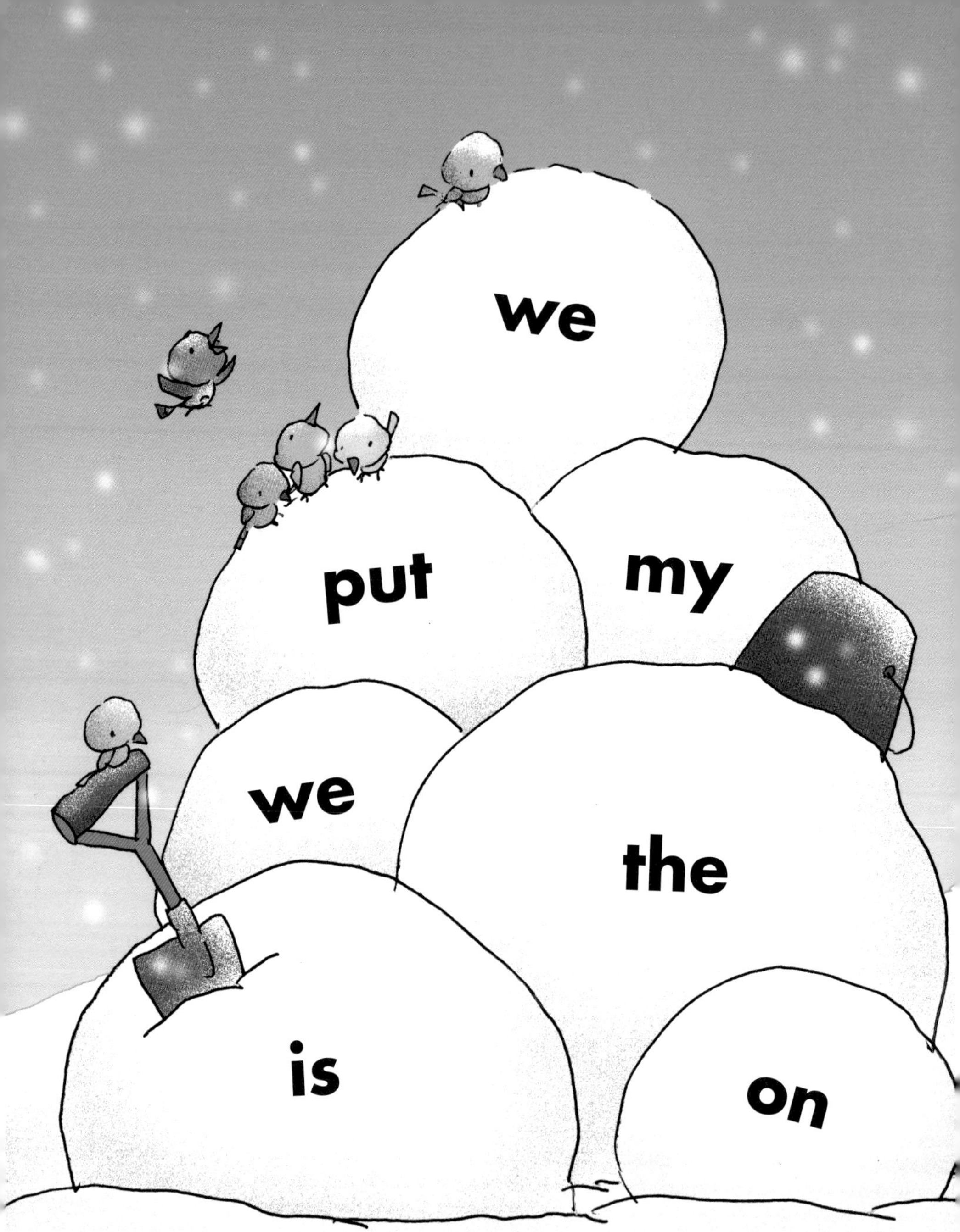
we
put
my
we
the
is
on